The Day We Lost Pet

BY CHUCK YOUNG

ILLUSTRATED BY ANIELA SOBIESKI

penny
candy
BOOKS

For Isabelle & Travie for always

Penny Candy Books
Oklahoma City & Savannah
Text © 2017 Chuck Young
Illustrations © 2017 Aniela Sobieski

The Sustainable Forestry Initiative® program integrates the perpetual growing and harvesting of trees with the protection of wildlife, plants, soils and water.

Design: Shanna Compton, shannacompton.com

Photo of Chuck Young by Bruce David Millet
Photo of Aniela Sobieski by Derek Engelking

21 20 19 18 17   1 2 3 4 5
ISBN-13: 978-0-9972219-9-2 (paperback)
ISBN-13: 978-0-9987999-3-3 (hardcover)

Books for the kid in *all* of us
www.pennycandybooks.com

In memory of

We

were just two balloon people in love then, inflated with the stardust that had held up Earth for millions of years.

Before that we were piles of skin laundry blending into a world of pales and fogs.

We don't remember how we met.
Except that I was a scientist surrounded by light bulbs,

and they were a florist stalked by pollen.
We had filament in common.

When we were together we noticed
that deflation happened quickly.

But also that we were inhaling each other.
And those breaths would hold us.

The essence that filled the both of us began
to blend; some of what blew out of me would
find new home within them, and the dry ice
of them would make nests within me.

Trying to make sense of this process
brought with it a new worry:

the possibility of total loss!

So we found a container and took turns putting the breeze
of us into that little orb until it took enough shape

to maintain its own space. It filled and filled with swirls
of light from the runoff of galaxy glow.

And somehow that balloon, of course, was you, Baby.

The three of us were made a
family. It felt like making room,
and it felt like expanding.

And we were happy.

The day the carnival came to town, we saw a sign
and couldn't believe our luck that someone
had figured out how to distribute star dirt
and space wind from a large tank.

We already knew about Mylar spheres that could float
up, up, up into space, eventually turning into planets.

But we had never heard of this: small balloons from a can
that became as alive as you or us but whose purpose
was to be kept on a string for companionship.

You loved Pet. And she went everywhere
with you. You breathed each other's air.
Some of her went into you and some
of you went into her. I'm sure of it.

But for some reason, Pet was deflating
at a speed we couldn't understand.

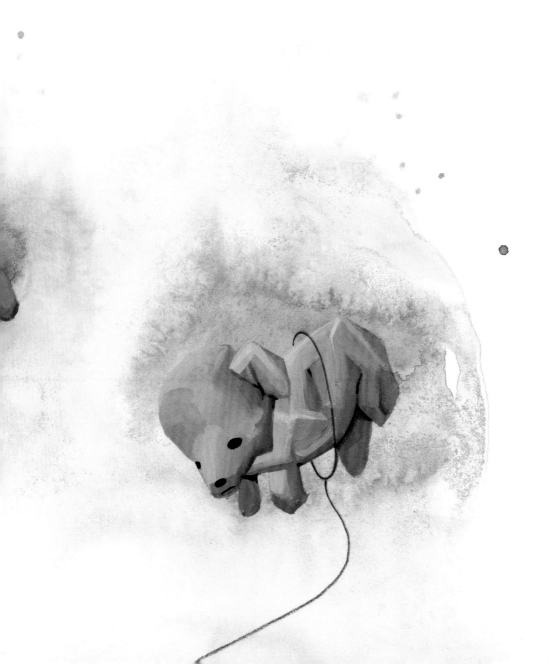

We went to work to find a solution.
We drifted apart to labs and woods.

Sometimes solving puzzles puts us
away from where we mean to be.

Separately buried inside the problem of
Pet disappearing, we failed to make the
most of our time together, to comfort you,
to do what it means to be a family.

For months, our only contact
was through dandelion-seed messages
bouncing across a shared sky

gone

until the day we read that we had lost Pet.
So we came back together as strangers.

And when you brought us the deflated bag of Pet,

we were reminded of what it meant to be here.

We decided that if all of what was inside
of her had gone into the atmosphere,

then we should dig a hole and put the fabric of her
into the land. Maybe she could again be chosen,
this time as a tree or a flutterby or a footprint.

You asked, "Which one is more her?
The skin husk or the spirit breath?"

We could see ourselves in the water of your eyes.

The good thing, Baby,
is that we knew the tank that birthed her
did not create the energy that filled her.

That tank harnessed the nothingness
of cosmic carbon and that
nothingness just *is*.

It is not created and therefore
can not be destroyed.

So we tell you now to remember the
fragrance of her small sighs. To pay closer
attention to long shadows. You will feel
her from time to time, we promise you.

You will breathe her in.

And in that vast expanse, you will learn
that forever can be its own kind of home.

CHUCK YOUNG lives and dads in his hometown of Clinton, Massachusetts. He was in a touring emo band, Orange Island, in the early 2000s and, more recently, managing editor of *theEEEL* by tNY.Press (a former channel of the *Los Angeles Review of Books*). He has published short fiction and poetry in various journals online and in print. *The Day We Lost Pet* is his first book.

ANIELA SOBIESKI is an artist from Minnesota. She earned a BFA in painting from the University of Wisconsin–Madison and an MFA from Syracuse University. Her artwork has been exhibited and collected both nationally and internationally. She lives with her husband and young daughter in St. Paul. *The Day We Lost Pet* is her debut as a children's book illustrator.